Elodie
the Lamb
Fairy

To Naomi O'Sullivan, who loves lambs

Special thanks to Rachel Elliot

The publisher does not have any control over and does not assume any responsibility for author or third-party websites or their content.

ISBN 978-1-338-20695-1

10 9 8 7 6 5 4 3 2 1   18 19 20 21 22

Printed in the U.S.A.   40
First printing 2018

Elodie
the Lamb
Fairy

by Daisy Meadows

SCHOLASTIC INC.

The Fairyland Palace

Farmhouse

Pond

Fluttering Fairyland Farm

Greenfields Farm

Greenfields House

Barn

Pond

I want a farm that's just for me,
With animals I won't set free.
It's far too slow to find each one.
Let fairy magic get this done!

With magic from the fairy farm,
I'll grant my wish—to their alarm!
And if I spoil the humans' fun,
Then Jack Frost really will have won!

Contents

Alarm on the Farm

COCK-A-DOODLE-DOO!

Kirsty Tate and Rachel Walker sat up in bed at exactly the same moment. For a few seconds, they couldn't figure out whcre they were. Then they remembered and shared an excited smile.

"You know you're on a farm when a rooster is your alarm clock," said Rachel, bouncing out of bed. "Quick, let's get dressed. I can't wait to say good morning to all the animals."

This was their first full day at Greenfields Farm, just outside Wetherbury, where they were going to spend all of spring break. The farm was owned by Harriet and Niall Hawkins, friends of Kirsty's parents, and they were getting ready to open it up to paying visitors at the end of the week. The Tates and Rachel had come to help them.

Kirsty slipped out of bed, too, and threw open the yellow curtains. The walls of the farmhouse were so thick that the windowsill was big enough to sit on. Kirsty put the blanket from her bed on the sill, and then perched there, gazing out over the farm. She could see the barn

where they had met Blossom the cow,
and the trees that hid the sparkling
duck pond. Over to the left, she could
see a green pasture, with sheep dotted
around it like little puffs of cotton
wool.

"It's going to be a lovely sunny day," said Rachel, joining her at the window. "This is perfect weather for working outside."

"I wouldn't mind rain or snow, as long as we get to spend the day with baby animals," said Kirsty with a smile.

The day before, the Hawkinses had asked the girls to look after the baby animals on the farm. Rachel and Kirsty were thrilled. They both loved animals, and they usually found that animals loved them, too.

As soon as the girls were dressed and had made their beds, they hurried down the creaky farmhouse stairs to the big kitchen. Niall and Harriet Hawkins were already there with the Tates.

"Good morning, you two," said Niall in

a cheerful voice. "You're just in time for
a big Greenfields Farm breakfast. Eggs
freshly laid this morning, milk and butter
from Blossom the cow, and hot, crusty
bread straight out of the oven."

"It sounds delicious," said Kirsty, her
stomach rumbling.

As the girls began to devour their food, Harriet went through her list of what needed to be done that day. She asked Mr. and Mrs. Tate to finish painting the welcome center, and then smiled at the girls.

"I've got a very special job for you to do this morning," she said. "Five lambs have been born here recently, and we want to get them used to bottle-feeding. The visitors will love being able to feed

lambs. Will you go to the sheep pasture after breakfast and bottle-feed the lambs?"

"We'd love to," said Rachel at once. "What a perfect way to start the day."

"Would you like me to come with you and show you how to do it?" Niall asked.

Rachel and Kirsty shook their heads.

"No, thank you," said Kirsty. "We've both bottle-fed lambs before. I'm sure we'll remember what to do."

"That's wonderful," said Harriet. "Thank you, Rachel and Kirsty."

"Thank you for letting us do it," said Rachel, smiling. "I love lambs—they're so soft and woolly. They're my favorite animal babies."

Kirsty laughed and squeezed her best friend's hand.

"You say that about all the animal babies," she told her.

"I know," said Rachel, also laughing. "I can never make up my mind. They're all so cute."

The girls had two fresh eggs each, followed by toast, butter, and homemade blackberry jam. They washed it all down with glasses of creamy, frothy milk, and then carried their plates to the sink.

"Thank you," said Harriet. "We'll finish tidying up in here. I've put a bucket of bottles next to the back door for the lambs. Do you know where the sheep pasture is?"

"Yes," said Kirsty. "We saw it from our bedroom window this morning."

"The lambs are in a pen beside the pasture," said Harriet. "See you later, girls."

Rachel and Kirsty pulled on their barn boots, and then Rachel picked up the bucket of bottles. They said good-bye to the grown-  ups and headed out toward the pasture.

To get there, they had to pass the barn. Blossom was outside, and she let out a happy moo as they walked past.

"Good morning, Blossom," said Rachel, going over to her and patting her side.

"We can't stop. We've got an important job to do this morning."

She held up the bucket of bottles, and Blossom mooed again.

"Yes, it's milk," said Kirsty. "See you later on, Blossom. We've got some animal babies to feed!"

Baa-Meow

The girls walked side by side up the path toward the sheep pasture. The morning breeze carried the fresh scent of grass to them, and they took deep breaths to drink it in.

"I wish I could live here," said Kirsty. "I love the countryside."

Rachel didn't reply. She was staring at something on the wooden pasture fence. It was an animal, and it was stepping carefully along the top railing.

"What *is* that?" she asked.

"A cat?" said Kirsty, sounding unsure.

"It looks too big for a cat," Rachel said.

They sped up, and as they got closer they went even faster. They could now see what the animal was, but neither of them could quite believe what was in front of their eyes.

"It's a lamb," said Kirsty in wonder. "I've never seen a lamb balancing on a fence before."

"I've never heard a lamb saying *meow*, either," said Rachel, frowning. "Listen."

As they got closer, Kirsty heard it, too. The lamb was meowing like a cat. The girls exchanged a worried glance.

"Jack Frost and his goblins are causing trouble again," said Kirsty. "I suppose we should have expected it after what happened yesterday."

The girls thought back to their adventures from the day before. They had been watching the new little ducklings on the Greenfields Farm pond, when Debbie the Duckling Fairy had fluttered out of a duck's nest. Rachel and Kirsty were used to finding fairies in unexpected places, so they were excited to meet her. They had been friends of Fairyland ever since they had met the Rainbow Fairies on Rainspell Island. They had been best friends since that day, too.

Debbie had taken them to see the animals at Fluttering Fairyland Farm, a magical farm that hovered in midair among the fluffy white clouds of Fairyland. There, the girls had met the other Farm Animal Fairies—Elodie the Lamb Fairy, Penelope the Foal Fairy, and Billie the Baby Goat Fairy. They had also seen the magical baby farm animals who helped the fairies look after baby farm animals everywhere. It had been one of the most amazing visits to Fairyland that Rachel and Kirsty could remember. But then Jack Frost had turned up with three of his mischievous goblins, and everything had gone terribly wrong.

Jack Frost wanted some cute, cuddly animals to make his own petting zoo at the Ice Castle. So far, he only had his snow goose and her baby, Snowdrop, and he wanted more. So he and his goblins had stolen the fairies' magical farm animals.

At once, Debbie had whisked the girls back to Greenfields Farm, where they

found that things were already going
wrong. The ducklings were acting like
puppies, including Splashy, Debbie's
magical duckling.

Thinking about their adventures the
day before, Rachel and Kirsty stared at
the meowing lamb.

"Jack Frost is responsible for this," said
Kirsty in a worried
voice. "Do you
think all the
lambs on the
farm are acting
like cats?"

"It might be
all the lambs in
the human world,"
Rachel replied.

"What will the Hawkinses say if they

come to see the lambs and find them like this?" said Kirsty.

"When we helped Debbie get Splashy back from the goblin who stole her, all the ducklings went back to normal," said Rachel. "We have to get Elodie's magical lamb back—then all the other lambs should be themselves again, too."

"We have to get *all* the missing magical animals back," said Kirsty. "Without them, Greenfields Farm will never be ready for visitors, and the farm babies will stay changed forever."

"You're right," said Rachel. "But first, let's get that lamb down from the fence."

Big Green Boots

Rachel put the bucket of bottles down.
Then, moving slowly and quietly, the girls
tiptoed up to the lamb.

"Hello," said Rachel in a gentle voice.
"What are you doing up here?"

She ran her hand along the lamb's
back. It opened its little mouth, but
instead of a bleat, it let out a loud meow.

"I wonder if it will let me pick it up,"
said Kirsty.

She tried to put her arms around it, but
the lamb leaped down from the fence
and scampered off. It moved more like a
cat than a lamb.

"Should we follow it?" Rachel said.
"No, wait," said Kirsty. "Look . . ."
She was staring at a little tuft of the
lamb's wool that was caught on the
fence. Rachel looked, too, and saw that

the wool had a faint glow to it. The glow
grew stronger and brighter, and then
the tuft of wool opened up like a flower.
There was a little burst of silver sparkles,
and, all at once, Elodie the Lamb Fairy
was sitting in the middle
of the wool with
her legs tucked
underneath
her. She was
wearing
a soft
pink dress
trimmed with
purple detailing,
and a fluffy lamb's-wool
vest. She clapped her hands when she saw
the girls, and her brown curls bounced
merrily up and down.

"I found you," she said with a smile. "Debbie told me how you helped her find Splashy. It's wonderful to have him back at Fluttering Fairyland Farm. Will you help me find Fluffy so that I can take her home, too?"

"We're always happy to help our fairy friends," said Rachel. "Oh, Elodie, you came at just the right time. We just saw a lamb acting like a cat."

"That doesn't sound good," said Elodie. "Right now I don't think *any* of the lambs in the human world are feeling normal. Where could the goblin be hiding Fluffy? As soon as I get her back home, all other lambs will start acting like lambs again."

"We'll help you look as soon as we've fed the farm's lambs," said Kirsty.

She picked up the bucket of bottles and Elodie fluttered inside it to hide. Then Rachel and Kirsty hurried up to the lambs' pen. But when they got there, just one lamb was inside. It was sitting up very straight, licking one of its hooves.

"Hello," said Rachel, stepping inside the pen. "Where are your friends, little lamb?

Where have they all gone?"

The lamb stood up, stretched, and then rubbed its face against Rachel's legs, just like a cat rubbing its whiskers. It started to purr, and when Kirsty came into the pen, it pressed against her legs, too. Then it weaved around both girls in a figure eight, still purring loudly.

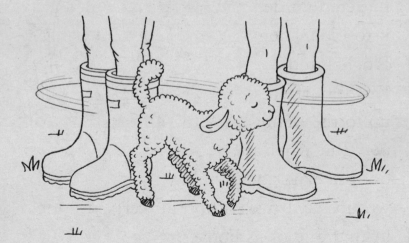

"You know, the goblins don't have a lot of imagination," said Rachel. "The one who took Splashy came here, and I bet the other two came here, too."

"I've got an idea," said Kirsty. "Elodie, if you turn us into fairies, we could fly over the farm to look for Fluffy and the other lambs. We'll be able to search a lot more quickly that way."

Elodie popped out of the bucket and glanced around. There were no other people in sight. She lifted her wand and did a little twirl in midair. Instantly, the girls felt themselves whirling around as they shrank to fairy size, and delicate wings unfurled on their backs.

They were scooped up on magical puffy clouds and swept into the air. The little lamb rose onto its hind legs to watch them. It batted at them with its front hooves, but the little clouds whisked them out of reach. Then the clouds melted away and Elodie joined them. Together, they zoomed up over the sheep pasture.

"Look down there," said Rachel. "The lambs are in the pasture."

Now that they had a good view, they

could see four lambs in the pasture. Two of them were rolling around together, play-fighting. Another lamb was busy chasing a leaf that was dancing in the breeze, pouncing on it and freeing it over and over again. The fourth lamb was scratching at the newly painted fence.

"It's just what we were afraid of," said Kirsty. "They're all acting like cats."

The lambs were meowing so loudly that the fairies could hear them clearly, even from high above. The sheep in the pasture were staying away from the lambs, and giving them some very confused looks. When the leaf-chasing lamb got too close, one of the sheep let out a loud, grumpy baa.

The lambs were startled by the loud noise. They all jumped up onto the pasture fence, balanced there for a moment, and then jumped down and ran off toward the farm.

"Oh no," said Kirsty. "How are we going to get them back?"

She and Elodie watched in a panic as the lambs scattered. Rachel was still looking all around, hoping to be lucky enough to spot Fluffy. There was no magical lamb in sight, but there was someone down in a grove of trees at the bottom of the pasture. He was wearing bright-green overalls and tall rubber boots, and he was looking up into a tree.

"Who is that?" Rachel asked. "It doesn't look like Niall. Are there any other people working on the farm this week, Kirsty?"

Kirsty looked where Rachel was pointing, and her mouth fell open.

"That's not a grown-up," she said. "It's not even a human. Look at his enormous boots. That's a goblin!"

Following the Trail

The goblin seemed to be calling to someone in the tree.

"Come on," said Elodie. "Let's go and find out what he's doing. He's one of Jack Frost's goblins, so I'll bet you anything he's up to mischief."

Rachel, Kirsty, and Elodie flew down toward the grove of trees. As they got closer, they saw a magical glow through the leaves.

"There's something in the tree," said Kirsty. "Oh, Elodie, I think it's Fluffy!"

The magical little lamb was balancing on a low branch. She looked alone and confused.

"Fluffy!" Elodie called.

Fluffy was startled, and she jumped down from the branch in a panic. She landed in the goblin's arms, and he gave a loud squawk of delight.

"You *do* want to cuddle me," he said. "You're so soft and sweet. I want more cuddles. I want *all* the cuddles!"

He squeezed her so tightly that she started to squirm and wriggle in his arms.

Seconds later, she twisted away from him and dashed off.

"Come back!" he shouted.

"Fluffy!" Elodie cried out.

The goblin charged after the little lamb, stumbling with every step he took in his massive boots. Fluffy pressed her belly to the grass and crawled under the shrubbery behind the grove of trees.

"We have to follow her," said Rachel, zooming into the greenery.

Elodie and Kirsty flew after her, but by the time they caught up, Fluffy had completely disappeared. They heard the goblin crashing into the bushes behind them.

Kirsty and Rachel looked at each other in dismay. How were they going to get Fluffy back now?

Rachel looked around and spotted a few tufts of Fluffy's wool clinging to the undergrowth.

"A trail," she said. "Maybe we can follow it. It might lead us to Fluffy, just like the breadcrumbs in the story *Hansel and Gretel*."

"That's a brilliant idea," said Elodie, clapping her hands together. "Quickly, there's not a moment to lose. We can't let Fluffy disappear again."

Staying low and flitting through the undergrowth, the fairies hunted for the little wisps of glowing white wool.

Here and there they found them clinging to twigs and caught on thorns. Rachel picked up each piece and held them all in her hand. The trail led them through the shrubbery, over to a bush, and when they peeked underneath it, they saw Fluffy curled up like a cat.

Elodie put her finger to her lips, and
they all backed away from the bush.

"We have to be very careful," she
whispered. "Now that we've found her,
we can't risk frightening her again."

"Maybe she would come with us if we
had a cat toy," said Kirsty, remembering
that they had used a toy to help them get
Splashy the duckling back.

Rachel looked down at the tufts of
Fluffy's glowing wool in her hand.

"Wool," she said. "That reminds me, cats love balls of yarn—they will chase them for hours. Could you make a ball of yarn, Elodie?"

Elodie flicked her wand, and instantly Rachel was holding a large ball of soft blue yarn.

"Perfect," said Rachel. "We will need to be human for this."

With another wave of her wand, Elodie turned the girls back into humans once again.

"This shrubbery suddenly seems a lot more cramped. And prickly," said Kirsty with a quiet laugh. "OK, Rachel, I'm ready. It's time to get Fluffy."

Rachel flashed her a thumbs-up.

Chase!

Kneeling down, Rachel rolled the ball of
yarn toward the little lamb, keeping hold
of one end of the yarn. The ball nudged
up against Fluffy's nose, and she opened
one eye. Kirsty and Rachel crossed their
fingers. But Fluffy just closed her eye
again. Rachel pulled the ball of yarn
back toward her.

"Let me try," said Kirsty.

She rolled the yarn ball and it bumped up against Fluffy's hoof. Again, one of her eyes flickered for a moment. But she was just not interested. Kirsty pulled the yarn back to herself.

The girls heard a rustling sound behind them. They turned around as a pair of green hands parted two bushes. The goblin stared at them through the shrubbery.

"What are *you* doing here?" he snapped.

He was glaring at Elodie—he hadn't yet noticed Fluffy under the bush. Trying to look casual,

Rachel edged sideways so that she was in front of the bush. The goblin looked at the ball of yarn.

"I'll take that," he said, reaching out and snatching it from Kirsty's hands. "I need it so I can take the lamb to Jack Frost's petting zoo at the Ice Castle."

"You can't just take things that don't belong to you," said Kirsty, pulling the yarn back.

"Give it to me!" the goblin squawked.

He scrambled toward her, and Kirsty jumped up and ran away, out of the grove of trees and toward the sheep pasture. Rachel glanced at Fluffy and noticed that the little lamb had opened her eyes. She had half raised her head, pricking up her ears.

"She's interested in the chase," Rachel said to Elodie, then cupped her hands around her mouth to call in a loud voice, "Kirsty, drop the end of the yarn!"

Kirsty didn't know why Rachel wanted her to drop the end of the yarn ball, but she trusted her best friend, so as she was running she unwound some of the

yarn and let it trail along the ground
behind her. The goblin, who was already
stumbling in his big rubber boots, now
tripped over the end of the yarn.

"Stop!" he screeched angrily. "Give me
that yarn!"

He pushed himself up again and kept running. Kirsty zigzagged around the bottom of the pasture, getting closer and closer to the shrubbery. Then, as fast as lightning, Fluffy suddenly darted out and pounced on the end of the yarn with a loud meow.

While Fluffy was busy patting the yarn string with her hoof, Rachel rushed forward and put her arms around the little

lamb. Elodie fluttered down and placed
one hand on Fluffy's back. Immediately,
Fluffy shrank to fairy size and let out a
loud baa.

"Hooray!"
Kirsty
cheered,
throwing
her arms
around
Rachel.
"Thank
goodness she's
a lamb again."

The goblin sank down on the grass and
rubbed his eyes.

"I only wanted to cuddle her and feel
her soft wool," he said in a sad voice.
"She's so sweet."

Elodie's face softened as she looked at the goblin. Rachel and Kirsty could tell that she felt sorry for him.

"There are other ways to enjoy the feel of a lamb's wool," said the little fairy in a gentle voice.

She waved her wand and a sweater appeared on the goblin's knee. It was bright green, and it looked as fluffy as a lamb. The goblin picked it up and pressed it against his cheek.

"This is the softest thing I've ever felt," he said.

He cuddled it and stroked it against his other cheek.

A big smile spread across his face.

"It's for you to keep," said Elodie.

The goblin jumped up and skipped away across the pasture.

"We should go back to the lambs' pen," said Kirsty. "Now that Fluffy is back with Elodie, all the little lambs should be back to normal."

"Let's go and find out," said Rachel.

The Magic of the Farm

The girls raced across the pasture to the pen, with Elodie zooming along in the air behind them. But when they reached the pen, they saw that there was still only one little lamb inside.

"At least it is behaving like a lamb again," said Rachel, watching him springing around the pen.

The girls stepped into the pen and the lamb trotted over to them, bleating with happiness. They stroked it, and it nuzzled them both.

"The other lambs must still be wandering around the farm," said Kirsty. "How are we going to find them and get them to come back here?"

"I don't know," said Kirsty, "but we *have* to find them. They are going to be one of the biggest attractions here on the farm."

"I'll use my magic," said Elodie. "Now that Fluffy is back with me, I will be able to bring the lambs back easily."

But just as she raised her wand, they all heard a high-pitched whistle coming from the direction of the farmhouse. They raised their hands to  shade their eyes from the sun and saw Harriet standing outside the barn. She blew her whistle again.

"What is she doing?" Rachel asked.

Just then, Patch the sheepdog appeared around the side of the barn, and in front of him were four white lambs. Elodie laughed in delight.

"I'll let the sheepdog take care of the lambs," she said. "It's time for me to take Fluffy back to the Fluttering Fairyland Farm."

She hovered beside Kirsty and dropped

a kiss on her cheek. Fluffy nuzzled
against her human friend, too. Then they
did the same to Rachel.

"Thank you both
for helping me find
Fluffy," Elodie said. "You're
wonderful. Without you, she
would still be meowing
and purring."

"We're just happy
that she's back where
she belongs," said
Kirsty.

Elodie smiled, and then she and Fluffy
disappeared in a puff of silvery sparkles.
Patch was just guiding the lambs up the
path, led by Harriet. Now that they were
closer, Rachel and Kirsty could hear the
lambs baaing in shrill voices.

Harriet opened the lambs' pen, and then Patch moved the lambs into it. He ran left and right, keeping low to the ground. His glossy black-and-white coat gleamed in the sunshine.

The last lamb skittered into the pen and Harriet closed the gate. Rachel and Kirsty hurried up to her.

"We're really sorry," said Kirsty at once.

"We were supposed to be taking care of the lambs, but they were already out of the pen when we arrived to feed them."

"Don't worry," said Harriet. "Patch has a magic touch with lambs. I can't imagine how they got out of the pen, though. It's not as if they could have jumped over the fence!"

Kirsty and Rachel shared a secret smile. What would Harriet have said if she had seen the lambs earlier?

The girls each took a bottle from the bucket and went into the pen. They knelt down and waited for the curious little lambs to come closer. Then they offered the bottles. Soon the girls were feeding the first two lambs, cuddling their soft, woolly coats as they drank their milk.

"Well," said Harriet with a laugh. "It looks as if you two have got a magic touch with the lambs as well. Come on, Patch. Let's leave Rachel and Kirsty to feed the lambs in peace."

As Harriet and Patch walked away, the girls exchanged happy smiles.

"Feeding lambs has to be one of the best feelings in the whole world," said Rachel. "I love them so much."

63

"Me, too," said Kirsty. "I just hope that we can help the two other Farm Animal Fairies get their magical animals back by the time Greenfields Farm opens for visitors."

"Everyone should have the chance to know the magic of caring for animals," said Rachel, smiling down at the little lamb she was feeding. "The fairies need us, and we won't let them down. I can't wait for our next magical adventure!"

RAINBOW magic
THE Farm Animal FAIRIES

Rachel and Kirsty have found Debbie's
and Elodie's missing magic animals.
Now it's time for them to help

Penelope
the Foal Fairy!

Join their next adventure in this
special sneak peek . . .

Poster Animals

"Just one day left until the farm's grand opening," said Kirsty Tate.

She was looking at a computer screen over the shoulders of Harriet and Niall Hawkins, the owners of Greenfields Farm. Her parents, Mr. and Mrs. Tate, and her best friend, Rachel Walker, were also gazing at the computer. They were all looking at the design for the new poster that would advertise the farm.

"I feel jumpy with excitement every time I think about the grand opening tomorrow," said Rachel.

"I feel jumpy with *nervousness* every time I think about it," said Harriet with a laugh. "I can't believe there's just one day left."

"I'm sure everything will be fine," said Mr. Tate, patting Harriet's shoulder.

The Tates and Rachel were all spending spring break at Greenfields Farm, just outside Wetherbury. The Tates were friends with Harriet and Niall, and they had all been helping to get the farm ready. Tomorrow, Greenfields Farm would open to visitors for the first time, complete with a children's petting zoo.

"You've all been wonderful," said Niall, turning in his chair to smile up at them. "Especially you, Rachel and Kirsty. We were worried about being too busy to look after the baby animals this week, but you've done everything for them."

"It's been a treat to look after them," said Kirsty with a smile.

Mr. Tate was still gazing at the poster design.

"I think it needs more photos of the farm," he said.

"How about adding some photos of the baby animals?" said Rachel. "They are so cute—they'd make anyone want to visit the farm."

"Especially animal lovers like us," Kirsty added.

"We could add some photos of the

foals," said Harriet. "They're really sweet—especially when they've just been groomed and are all nice and clean."

"I saw them this morning and they are definitely not clean at the moment," said Niall with a chuckle. "I've never seen such scruffy looking foals before. Girls, would you mind giving the foals a bath and grooming them before they have their photo taken?"

Rachel and Kirsty exchanged a glance of pure delight.

"That sounds like so much fun," said Rachel. "We'd love to do it."

RAINBOW magic

Which Magical Fairies Have You Met?

- ❏ The Rainbow Fairies
- ❏ The Weather Fairies
- ❏ The Jewel Fairies
- ❏ The Pet Fairies
- ❏ The Sports Fairies
- ❏ The Ocean Fairies
- ❏ The Princess Fairies
- ❏ The Superstar Fairies
- ❏ The Fashion Fairies
- ❏ The Sugar & Spice Fairies
- ❏ The Earth Fairies
- ❏ The Magical Crafts Fairies
- ❏ The Baby Animal Rescue Fairies
- ❏ The Fairy Tale Fairies
- ❏ The School Day Fairies
- ❏ The Storybook Fairies
- ❏ The Friendship Fairies

■ SCHOLASTIC

Find all of your favorite fairy friends at
scholastic.com/rainbowmagic

HIT entertainment

RMFAIRY17

RAINBOW magic™

SPECIAL EDITION

Which Magical Fairies Have You Met?

- ❏ Joy the Summer Vacation Fairy
- ❏ Holly the Christmas Fairy
- ❏ Kylie the Carnival Fairy
- ❏ Stella the Star Fairy
- ❏ Shannon the Ocean Fairy
- ❏ Trixie the Halloween Fairy
- ❏ Gabriella the Snow Kingdom Fairy
- ❏ Juliet the Valentine Fairy
- ❏ Mia the Bridesmaid Fairy
- ❏ Flora the Dress-Up Fairy
- ❏ Paige the Christmas Play Fairy
- ❏ Emma the Easter Fairy
- ❏ Cara the Camp Fairy
- ❏ Destiny the Rock Star Fairy
- ❏ Belle the Birthday Fairy
- ❏ Olympia the Games Fairy
- ❏ Selena the Sleepover Fairy

- ❏ Cheryl the Christmas Tree Fairy
- ❏ Florence the Friendship Fairy
- ❏ Lindsay the Luck Fairy
- ❏ Brianna the Tooth Fairy
- ❏ Autumn the Falling Leaves Fairy
- ❏ Keira the Movie Star Fairy
- ❏ Addison the April Fool's Day Fairy
- ❏ Bailey the Babysitter Fairy
- ❏ Natalie the Christmas Stocking Fairy
- ❏ Lila and Myla the Twins Fairies
- ❏ Chelsea the Congratulations Fairy
- ❏ Carly the School Fairy
- ❏ Angelica the Angel Fairy
- ❏ Blossom the Flower Girl Fairy
- ❏ Skyler the Fireworks Fairy
- ❏ Giselle the Christmas Ballet Fairy
- ❏ Alicia the Snow Queen Fairy

■ SCHOLASTIC

Find all of your favorite fairy friends at
scholastic.com/rainbowmagic

3 stories in each one!

HIT entertainment

RMSPECIAL20